For
Matilda, Marigold
and
Skritty Kitty (of course!)

First published 2012 by Macmillan Children's Books
This edition published 2013 by Macmillan Children's Books
a division of Macmillan Publishers Limited
20 New Wharf Road, London N1 9RR
Basingstoke and Oxford
Associated companies throughout the world
www.panmacmillan.com
www.emilygravett.com

ISBN: 978-1-4472-1862-3

3 5 7 9 8 6 4 2

A CIP catalogue record for this book is available from the British Library.

Printed in China

Matilda's Cat

Emily Gravett

Macmillan Children's Books

Matilda's cat likes playing with wool,

~~playing with wool,~~
boxes,

~~playing with wool,~~

~~boxes,~~

and riding bikes!

Matilda's cat likes
tea parties,

~~tea parties,~~

funky hats,

~~tea parties,~~
~~funky hats,~~
and fighting foes!

Matilda's cat likes drawing.

~~drawing,~~

climbing trees,

~~drawing,~~

~~climbing trees,~~

and bedtime stories.

Matilda's cat does NOT like
playing with wool,
boxes,
riding bikes,
tea parties,
funky hats,
fighting foes,
drawing,
climbing trees,
OR bedtime stories.

Matilda's cat likes...

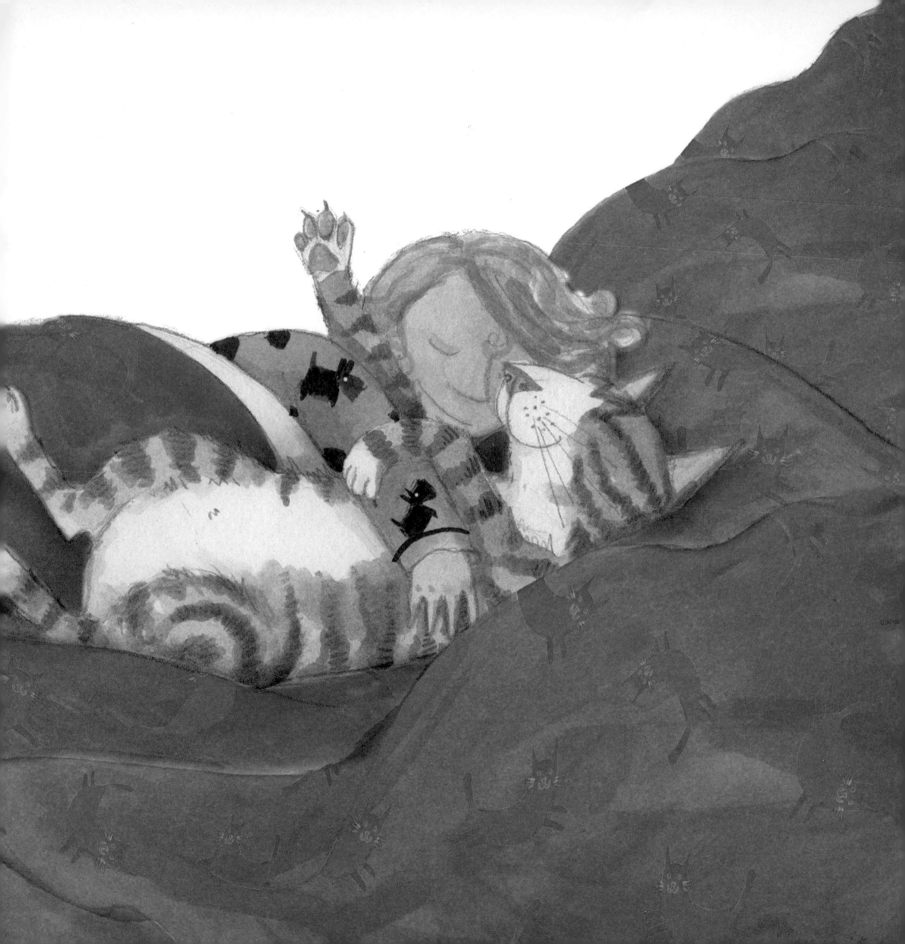